TOBY TUCKER

Picking People's Pockets

Also by Val Wilding

Toby Tucker: Keeping Sneaky Secrets
Toby Tucker: Dodging the Donkey Doo
Toby Tucker: Sludging through a Sewer
Toby Tucker: Mucking about with Monkeys
Toby Tucker: Hogging all the Pig Swill

A huge thank you to the wonderful Milestones –
Hampshire's Living History Museum, Basingstoke,
for being so helpful and accommodating.

www.milestones-museum.com

TOBY TUCKER

Picking People's Pockets

VAL WILDING

Illustrated by Michael Broad

EGMONT

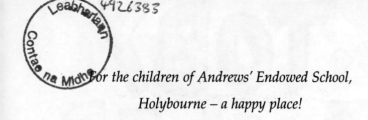
EGMONT

We bring stories to life

Published in Great Britain 2007
by Egmont UK Limited
239 Kensington High Street, London W8 6SA

Text copyright © 2007 Val Wilding
Cover and illustrations copyright © 2007 Michael Broad

The moral rights of the author and illustrator have been asserted

ISBN 978 1 4052 1837 5

1 3 5 7 9 10 8 6 4 2

A CIP catalogue record for this title is available
from the British Library

Printed and bound in Great Britain by the CPI Group

The Allen house, present day

Toby Tucker was bursting to get back upstairs and open his wooden chest again. He dumped his two wet dogs in the garden and went in the kitchen door. He sniffed. 'What's that yummy smell?'

His foster mother, Evie, took a baking tray out of the oven. 'Flapjacks,' she said. 'You can have one when they cool a bit. Good walk?'

'Barney and Snowball went in the pond.' Toby leaned hungrily over the tray. 'Barney walked in, and it only came up to his tummy, but Snowball

did her famous belly flop. She's covered in green slime. I'll hose her off later.'

'Well, do it near my veg patch,' said Evie. 'Save me a job. Speaking of jobs, where's Don? It's nearly ten o'clock.'

'I'm here!' said Toby's foster father from the doorway. 'Popped out to get new bath taps.'

'Well, when you've fixed those, you're coming to the supermarket,' said Evie. 'Then you can make a start on the downstairs loo ceiling.'

Decorating their house had been a non-stop task since Don and Evie Allen had moved in, just before Toby came to live with them.

Don sniffed. 'What's that?'

Toby pointed. 'Flapjacks! Can't wait for them to cool.'

'What? You're going to eat them?' Don shook his head. 'You do know that they use those to test the biting strength of false teeth, don't you?'

Evie glared at him. As he left the kitchen, a wet dishcloth caught him on the back of the neck!

Toby giggled, grabbed a flapjack and went up to his bedroom at the very top of the house. He wished Don and Evie would hurry up and get round to doing his room. They'd made it really nice for when he moved in from the children's home, but they hadn't had time to get rid of the hideous wallpaper. Pink! Fairies! Toby hated it, and he'd never let his best friends Jake and Amber come upstairs.

He knew they thought he was weird and secretive. It wasn't just the wallpaper, though that really was just so embarrassing. Toby did have a secret. A big one!

He knelt by the wooden chest that stood beneath the window. Apart from his clothes and a few bits and pieces, it was the only possession he'd brought from the children's home. And it held the secret – a secret he didn't know how to explain to anyone.

'To-by!'

Oh no! Amber! And she was on her way up!

'Toby! Where are you?'

He bounded down the stairs. 'Hi, Amber, I'm just coming down.' He blocked the way.

Amber held a half-eaten slice of flapjack. 'Mrs Allen thought you were in the sitting room, but you weren't,' she said, 'so I came to find you. Jake might be round later.'

'Great,' said Toby. 'Let's go out. Snowball will be glad to see you.'

'I'm supposed to be going to the paper shop for my dad.' Amber wiped crumbs from her mouth. 'That was great,' she sighed. 'Wish my mum could cook like yours.'

Toby was going to say, 'She's not exactly my mum,' but he didn't. What Amber said sounded nice.

Barney scavenged for flapjack crumbs, while Snowball rolled over for Amber to tickle her filthy tummy.

'I came to tell you I'm off tomorrow afternoon for the weekend,' said Amber. 'We're all going

camping,' she explained. 'We go every year. We meet up with another big family, so it's really fun.'

She checked her watch. 'Better go. See ya.'

'See ya.' Toby saw her out, then headed up to his room again, and the wooden chest.

Evie passed him on the stairs. 'Toby, love, we really will start your room just as soon as we can, though I don't imagine Amber would mind the fairies at all. She might even like them.'

Toby laughed. 'Doubt it! She's got footballers all over hers.'

'What? Wallpaper?'

'Posters – loads of them!'

'I see,' said Evie, carrying on down the stairs. 'You know, you could always make a start on the decorating yourself, if you wanted to.'

Toby leaned over the banister. 'Haven't got time.'

She laughed. 'Still struggling with that jigsaw of a family tree, eh?'

Toby nodded. 'Still struggling!' He went into his room. Seconds later, in came Evie. 'I forgot to tell you, I've been in touch with the children's home again – they still can't throw any light on the old question.'

Together, they chorused, 'Who's Toby Tucker?' and laughed.

Toby was quiet for a moment. If you only knew, he thought. There are times – magical times

– when you shouldn't be asking, 'Who's Toby Tucker?', you should be asking, 'Where's Toby Tucker?'

'Look,' he said, going to his pinboard. 'I've got four names now.'

'You know quite a lot about your ancestors already,' said Evie. 'More than I do about mine! Right, we're off to the supermarket. Will you hang out the washing if we're not back by the time the machine stops? It'll be about an hour.'

'Sure.' Toby glanced up again at his ancestors' names. Don and Evie, he thought, have no idea exactly how much I do know about my ancestors. And today, I hope to find out more.

From the hall downstairs, Toby heard Don grumbling about having to go shopping, then, when the front door shut, he put a CD on really loud and opened his wooden chest.

Beneath the mountain of paper scraps inside it, was a framed photo. Toby looked forward to the warm feeling he always got when he saw the gentle face of the elderly man in the photo. Was he one of Toby's ancestors?

On the back of the frame was a pencilled note.

> The paper in the chest is your family tree. I wonder which little baby tore it up, eh, Toby Tucker? Piece it together and you'll find out who you are and when you come from.
>
> Gee.

Toby knew, from experience, that Gee, whoever he was, hadn't made a mistake. He actually did mean 'when you come from', not 'where'.

That was the secret the chest held. All Toby had to do to start the magic was piece together a name from the scraps in the box. He'd done it four times already, when he found the names on his pinboard. How could he ever explain to anyone the amazing truth, that he actually became those people – that, for a while, he lived their lives?

Toby took out two great handfuls, settled

8

down on his deep red carpet, and began sorting through them.

'Pel . . . ates . . . Lar . . .'

Nothing there.

He got excited when he found 'rick', thinking that was a name by itself, but quickly realised it wasn't, because it didn't have a capital letter.

'Per . . . Trott . . .' Toby punched his fist in the air. 'Trott! Yesss!'

He heard footsteps on the stairs. 'Don?' he called. 'Did she let you off the hook, then?' He looked up to see not Don, but Jake!

'Hi, Toby! The door was unlocked, but there was no one downstairs, and I called, but your music was too loud . . .'

His voice trailed away as he gazed round the room. 'Blimey!'

Toby felt hot. 'I didn't choose it,' he said. 'They keep promising to get rid of it, but – you know. Don told me I could start it myself, but it'll take too long. They're quite quick at decorating – once they get started.'

Jake threw himself on the bed. 'What are you doing?'

'Nothing.' Toby picked up all the bits of paper except the one with 'Trott' on it, and thrust them back in the chest. 'Want to come to the cinema with us tomorrow evening?'

Jake shook his head. 'I can't, sorry. It's my aunt's fortieth birthday and she's having a big family party. We're going.'

Toby made a face. 'Bor-ing. Loads of old people.'

'It'll be great,' said Jake. 'All my cousins are going.'

'So?'

'Cousins are brilliant!' said Jake. 'They're like brothers and sisters, only you don't have to live with them.' He jumped off the bed and looked round once more at the wallpaper. 'Blimey!' And he was gone.

Toby heard the back door shut. He glared at the wallpaper. Then he marched towards the corner by the window, reached up and picked at a tiny, turned-down edge.

Sheeeeesh!

He ripped off nearly a whole sheet of the horrible, shiny wallpaper and flung it to the floor. 'Flipping fairies!' he shouted.

Feeling slightly better, he went back to 'Trott'. He thought he'd picked up all the other pieces, but there was one left. He turned it over. It said, 'Alfie'.

'Oh wow! I wonder.' Toby crouched down and slid 'Alfie' towards 'Trott'. The two pieces fitted together exactly. Instantly, a drawing started to appear. It was a boy in an old-fashioned shirt, trousers and a cap. Toby knew from experience that this was Alfie Trott. Almost as soon as it was complete, the drawing morphed into a picture of . . .

'Me. It's me,' Toby breathed, his heart galloping as he watched his own portrait change back into the boy in the cap. As soon as it did, the picture began to shimmer with a silvery light. The light grew into a shining column, half as high as Toby's room. It moved towards him, passed over him, and as it did he felt as if he'd swallowed cold jelly, and it was slithering all through his body. He thought to himself, He'll be there when I look, right where my chest should be.

Toby stood and turned. Yes, the boy was there, his back to the room. A mysterious force, like the pull of a giant magnet, tugged Toby towards him.

Toby didn't fight the force. He was too excited. Where was he going? *When* was he going?

'Watch it!' he shouted. 'I –' He never finished. His right foot found the torn sheet of wallpaper. The shiny surface slid on the carpet, taking Toby with it. His feet went from beneath him and he slipped straight into the boy.

He landed on his bottom. 'Ow! That's cold!'

Cold? Where was he? *Who* was he? Rubbing his wet behind he got up carefully, then picked up the bread.

Bread? Of course. It's my bread, he thought. I got it for Ma. My ma. Alfie Trott's ma.

I'm Alfie Trott.

What a start to the New Year! I slipped on a patch of ice, sat in a pool of slush and dropped Ma's loaf of bread in the gutter. It cleaned up nicely with a bit of spit, though, and she never noticed.

I say I slipped, but I reckon someone pushed me. I heard a voice shout 'Watch it!' and the next thing, I felt a thump in my back. Course, the blighter who did it had scarpered by the time I looked round. It made me woozy for a minute, though. Happy New Year, Alfie Trott!

I don't suppose this year will be any different from all the others. Pa keeps promising he's going to change our lives. I just wish he'd change the lock on our door, so people couldn't sneak in and out whenever they want to. Some kid was in here for a whole day last week before anyone noticed he wasn't one of ours.

There's nine of us in this family. Ma moans a lot about living in one room. She used to live in a house with two rooms upstairs and two rooms downstairs, she says. Sounds like a flipping palace to me! Imagine being in a room on your own!

She's always telling me, 'If only you could get educated, then you could be someone – have a real job.'

I don't know what she's going on about. I am someone. I'm Alfie – Alfie Trott. And I will have a real job, 'cos Pa's training me. At least, that's what he says he's doing.

His hands can slip in and out of a toff's pocket like an eel through water.

Pa doesn't need to be tall and strong for what he does. He has to be quick and quiet. One day I'll be as good as him – or better. I'm going to be the best pickpocket in town! And I'll never get caught. Pa got caught once, but he elbowed the copper in the ribs and got away. Ma nearly went berserk when he told her. 'If you get caught we've all had it!' she cried.

It takes a lot to make Ma cry. We haven't got much, but that day she managed to throw everything we have got. At Pa.

❧ ❧ ❧

Last night, young Billy was sick on my bit of the bed, so I wrapped myself up in all the spare clothes I could find and curled up on the floor. I couldn't sleep, so I did some thinking.

Ma says all Pa's good for is keeping the wolf from the door. Hah! If he can't keep out the odd stray kid, he won't have much luck with wolves. I know what she really means – Pa only just manages to earn enough to feed us.

Ma gets our clothes by selling the ones we've all grown out of, and buying bigger ones from the second-hand shop. You can get anything to wear there. We sometimes buy rags which Ma turns into clothes. Once we lost my smelliest sister in the shop. We found her in a huge pile of rags just outside the door. Ma said the rags were full of fleas and told her off good and proper. That night my sister did a wee in Pa's boot. He said we should have left her to the fleas.

Anyway, what I thought was that if Pa can't change our lives, maybe I can?

Went to work with Pa today. We have to walk quite a long way before we start. We never work near where we live. I don't know why.

I do get fed up, because Pa never lets me have a go myself. How can he train me if I never do a job?

I watch him, to learn what to do. So that people can't see what his hand's up to, Pa moves close to his mark – that's the victim who's going to have his pocket picked. We've got a system. Once Pa's nicked something he passes it to me. That's so if he's ever caught, he won't have stolen stuff on him, then he can't get done for pickpocketing.

Although I moan a lot, we do make a good team. Pa presses on the mark's back with one hand, and dips his pocket with the other. The mark feels the pressure on his back and doesn't notice what's going on elsewhere. I'm the

crow. That means I stand around looking innocent. If I see a peeler, I whistle to warn Pa.

The instant Pa's done the job, I move nearer, but I never stop watching to see if he's been spotted. If he has, he drops what he's nicked, and legs it. Then I stand around going, 'Ain't it shocking?' or 'You can't trust nobody these days, can you?'

Pa slips the watch to me and I tuck it inside my jacket and wander off. Then we meet up and see what we've got. Well, what Pa's got – he never gives me nothing.

Today I asked Pa, like I do every day, when I can have a go at dipping. He told me I'm nowhere good enough yet, so I can get that idea out of my stupid noddle.

Well, he's wrong, ain't he? I've been practising. I told him I'd picked his own pocket that morning, and showed him his matchbox. 'How d'you do that?' he said.

I told him I did it while Ma was screeching at us to get out from under her feet – that racket would cover the blast of a volcano, never mind the rattle of a matchbox. I thought it would buck Pa up, but it didn't. He boxed my ears and said, 'Never dip my pockets again.'

He still won't let me have a proper go. Probably thinks I'm useless. So I've decided. As soon as I get a chance, I'm going to pick someone's pocket myself. That'll show him I ain't such a duffer.

No work today. Ma says it's wrong to work on Sunday. Instead we went down to the river. She only takes us down there in winter because, she reckons, the sewage in the water doesn't stink like it does when the weather's hot.

The wind was freezing, but we were wrapped up nice and warm. When we smelled

the hot potato man, we all sniffed really loud so Pa knew we wanted some. Our noses were running, so the sniffing was really horrible. Ma said we were disgusting and to leave off, and Pa said, 'All right, have a potato.' We had one between two, with butter and salt, so Pa must have done OK this week.

In the afternoon, Ma told us to go out and play, so four of us played this game where you throw a ball at someone's legs. If you hit them, they get the ball and try to hit your legs. We haven't got a ball, so we made one out of rags. Then someone's scabby dog ran off with it, so we used a stone. It really hurt.

When I went to bed, I curled up tight and made a plan. I like making plans. I'd just got it all sorted in my mind when Billy threw himself over and sat on my head. It's quite hard to plan a crime with a bottom on your ear.

Today was the day I put my plan into operation. OK, I got into trouble, but it was worth it. This is what happened. I worked with Pa until two o'clock. He bought me a hot pie before he went to the pub for his dinner and ale.

I said I was going for a walk. 'Behave yourself,' Pa said. 'I don't want no lad of mine getting into trouble.'

I headed for the river and along the bank, towards where we live, then turned off into a busy street with loads of shops. I pretended to look in windows, but really I was looking for a likely mark. Suddenly, a tall man sneezed. He pulled out a black silk hanky and gave his snitch a good wipe. Then he shoved the hanky in his pocket.

But not quite. One little end was sticking out. And that silk hanky was worth a few bob.

I moved close to the mark. My tummy fluttered. Now or never. Now, I decided!

Swish! The hanky was up my sleeve before you could say, 'Nick it quick'. And I was gone. I stopped at the first pawnbroker's shop I found.

I'd folded the hanky carefully so the pawnbroker didn't see the snotty bits. He stroked it. 'Nice silk,' he mumbled. 'Give yer a penny.' Cheek! He could sell that for a shilling. Just because I'm a kid! Pa would have got more.

My first earnings, all of my own! OK, it's not much, but it's a start.

As I took the coin, a fat pasty-faced bloke with ginger side-whiskers dug me with his elbow, and winked. 'Where d'you get that wiper, eh?' he asked, pointing to the hanky. 'It's my pa's,' I said. Pa says never tell anyone anything they don't need to know.

'Hah!' said Ginger. 'You nicked it, didn't you?' He thought I was a proper professional pickpocket. I grinned proud-ly. But his face changed and went all hard. 'Where?' he growled. 'Better not be from round here. This is Mr Barkitt's patch, this is.'

I didn't hang around to find out what had got him in a stew. I scarpered!

Pa was waiting when I got to the pub. I skid-ded to a stop and met a faceful of beery breath. 'Where've you been?' he bawled. 'I told . . .' His voice croaked as he looked over my shoulder. At the corner stood Ginger, arms folded. He looked at us, long and hard, then walked away. Pa was quiet all the way home.

Seeing Ginger must have given Pa something to think about, because he forgot to ask me where I'd been. We didn't go out to work yesterday. I don't know why. When Ma had a go at Pa for being lazy, he said he was lying low for a bit. Huh! I know all about lying low. When your bed's the floor you can't lie much lower!

So I had to wait till today to practise dipping

again. While Pa was in the pub, I wandered off to a market. A costermonger's barrow bumped over a broken cobble, and a dozen cooking apples rolled off. 'I'll get 'em,' I said, and picked them all up.

The costermonger was so pleased he gave me an apple that was too bruised to sell. I put it in my pocket, next to the one I'd already nicked as I was picking them up. Quite a meal today, even if they were a bit sour!

I didn't go to the street where I'd dipped the hanky. I went round the corner where there were tall houses facing a park. People were standing

round a hokey pokey boy. I thought I might dip one of them.

Even though it was cold, everyone wanted to taste the creamy ice the hokey pokey boy sells. Ma says it's disgusting using the same glass as complete strangers. She ought to tell that to Pa and his mates down the pub.

Before I reached the crowd, a maid came up the area steps of a big, posh house. She had some stuff wrapped in cloths in her basket. One long thing stuck out. I threw my apple core away and moved close behind her.

I had a quick look round to make sure no one was watching and – whish! It was inside my jacket. I nipped round the corner and had a look at my trophy.

It was a silver knife! My second dip and I'd scored! For a moment I wondered if the maid would get into trouble, but I reckon there must be hundreds of silver knives in that house. I headed for the pawnbroker's. Best to get rid of it straight away.

'Hmm. Nice,' he said. 'But broken.'

The maid must have been taking it for repair.

'It's good silver,' I said.

'I'll give it a shine, so I can see it properly,' said the pawnbroker, going through to the back of the shop. Next second a kid scooted out of there and ran past me.

'Won't be a minute,' called the pawnbroker. I leaned on the counter like I've seen Pa do, and looked around.

Suddenly I felt such a thump in the middle of my back I thought my teeth would shoot out of my mouth. I turned. It was Ginger!

'You get off of Mr Barkitt's patch, you little guttersnipe,' he bawled, 'or it'll be the worse for you, and no mistake.'

No one, no one, shoves Alfie Trott around. 'I don't give a tinker's cuss for Mr Barkitt,' I shouted. 'Or you!'

His face screwed up in fury and he dived at me. But I was too fast. I took off like a cat out of a nest of rats.

It was only when Pa clipped me round the ear again for being late that I realised I didn't get my money, and I'd left the knife behind. Well, that's it. I'm never going there again.

I really got the shivers today. Twice. Pa and I had a good morning and he bought me dinner – proper dinner with a chop and gravy. While he had a glass of ale or two (or three, judging by the state of him later), I went off dipping.

At least that was the idea. I headed for a street where there are lots of shops and was looking for a mark when I heard, 'Stop! Thief!'

I was just about to do a runner when I realised it couldn't be me they were shouting at. I hadn't done anything! Then I saw a peeler arrest a kid, smaller than me.

The poor kid didn't

half get what-for. The peeler was hopping mad. 'Have a dip on my beat, would yer?' Thump! 'You'll get the birch for this, my lad.' Thump!

On that very spot, I swore never to pick another pocket in the whole of my life. I've heard all about the birch from people who've had it, and I don't ever want it.

I watched the peeler take the kid away. He was screaming his head off. The kid I mean, not the peeler. And I don't blame him.

That was the first shiver. As I said, I swore never to pick another pocket, but I soon broke my vow. A crowd watching something exciting is the best time for pickpockets to work. Their attention's on something else, and with all the pushing and shoving, they never notice a couple of fingers, like scissors, sliding into their pocket.

I was just dipping a nicely bulging pocket when something gripped my neck. For a moment

I thought a lion from the Zoological Gardens had got me. I felt hot breath on my ear, but it wasn't a lion. My stomach scrunched up – a peeler!

I whipped my hand out of the pocket, and froze. A hoarse voice whispered, 'I told you to stay off Mr Barkitt's patch. Didn't I?' As he said, 'Didn't I?' he shook me by the neck. I was stretched so tall and thin I thought I'd lose my trousers.

The owner of the fat pocket was smirking at me. Fool didn't know how near he'd come to being robbed!

The man spun me round. It was Ginger!

'How do I know when I'm in Mr Barkitt's patch?' I gasped.

'You make it your business to find out,' he snarled. As he let go of my neck he grabbed at the front of my shirt, but I was off! I ran like I've never run before, straight back to my pa.

I'm never going back on Mr Barkitt's patch again.

It seemed like I'd only just got off to sleep last night, but it was dawn when our whole building got woken up by hammering on doors and voices shouting at each one, 'Trott! You in there?' Finally they reached our door and before Pa could get his long johns on, Ginger burst in.

Ma started screaming about how she told Pa to fix that lock, and he told her to hold her tongue and pushed her, so she started bawling and what with all the kids howling, Ginger could hardly make himself heard. He pulled Pa out on to the landing.

Everything went quiet, then Pa came back in. All he said was, 'You and me have got to have a little talk.'

I don't really want to remember that talk. Pa knows about me doing jobs of my own. He also knows I was warned off Mr Barkitt's patch, and that I took no notice. It seems Mr Barkitt's more important than I thought. He's the bigwig around here – even the peelers leave him alone. And I told Ginger I didn't give a tinker's cuss for him!

My whole life changed today. My family must hate me, I reckon.

Last night we went to Mr Barkitt's place, and I nearly died when I saw him.

Mr Barkitt was the bloke with the fat pocket. The one Ginger caught me dipping!

The long and the short of it was that Mr Barkitt told Pa he wasn't having people living on his patch who interfered with his businesses. 'My people do the dipping – not that little guttersnipe!' (He meant me.)

'He won't do it ever again,' Pa promised.

'Dead right, he won't,' said Mr Barkitt. 'I own the building you live in, and you can all get out. Today!'

Pa begged him not to throw us out. 'It'll be the workhouse for me and the missus and all our littl'uns,' he said in a whiny voice.

That gave me the willies. Nobody wants to go to the workhouse – you get horrible food that

looks like sick, and you have to work till you're worn out, even little kids.

'Please, Mr Barkitt, let us stay,' Pa said. 'How can you think of separating the littl'uns from their Ma?'

I know why he said that. When families go in the workhouse, they get split up. Men, women and children all go in separate places. They only see each other once a week.

Mr Barkitt looked at me and jerked his head towards the door. I didn't need telling twice. I shot out and cannoned straight into a muffin seller, setting her bell jangling. Her basket tipped up and all her muffins hit the ground. I shouted, 'Sorry!' and ducked, expecting a clip round the ear. But she glanced at Mr Barkitt's door and said, 'Never mind, lad. Accidents happen.'

Eh?

I helped her pick up the muffins. She flicked some dirt off one and handed it to me. 'Here, lad. Any friend of Mr Barkitt is a friend of mine. A bit of dirt won't hurt the nobs.'

Pa came out just then. When he saw my muffin, he roared, 'Don't you ever learn? Don't steal on Mr Barkitt's patch.'

'I didn't,' I said. 'She give it me!'

'Think I'm stupid?' he snapped, and clipped me round the ear. Then he snatched my muffin and ate it. I hope it had something nasty on it.

'Have we got to move?' I asked.

'No, we haven't,' he said. 'You have. Mr Barkitt's letting us stay – on condition he never sets eyes on you again.'

So I've been sent to live with Ma's sister in Shepherd's Bush, on the other side of the city. Aunt Ivy's posh. And she and Uncle Bert aren't pleased to see me. Nor is their horrible dog, Tinker. I've given the rotten smelly beast a new name – Stinker.

Wash! Wash! Wash! That's all Aunt Ivy's made me do this last week. I wasn't here two minutes and I found myself stark naked, up to my belly

button in hot water. I haven't had all my clothes off in one go since I was a nipper.

Aunt Ivy scrubbed me with a brush – she said it'll take weeks to get the filth off me. She has her bath in front of the fire, all cosy like, and I have to go outside.

Uncle Bert says he wouldn't get in the bath if you paid him. (You can tell.)

He reckons it's a waste of good coal, heating water for a 'young guttersnipe' like me. Cheek! Uncle Bert's so mean. He doesn't even pay for the coal. He brings it home from the coal yard. That's what he does. He's a coalman. It's a filthy job. I know, because he makes me go out on the cart with him, delivering sooty black sacks of the stuff. I call him Uncle Dirt – just to myself, of course. I ain't barmy.

Aunt Ivy and Uncle Dirt think they're better than my family, just because they've got a whole house. It's huge. They've got a front room which you can only sit in when you're clean. Stinker isn't allowed in there, thank heavens. That dog hates me.

Aunt Ivy and Uncle Dirt have got so many things, and they all belong to them! There's a little china dish that's not for putting things in – it just sits there. I asked where they nicked it, and found myself up the stairs so fast I almost left my boots behind.

They've got three books. Three! Blimey, they're posh. One's the Bible. I know, because it's got a cross on it. I don't know what the other two

are. Aunt Ivy won't let me touch. She says I'll spoil them. How can you spoil books just by looking at them? I thought that's what books are for. I've got a new name for her. Poison Ivy.

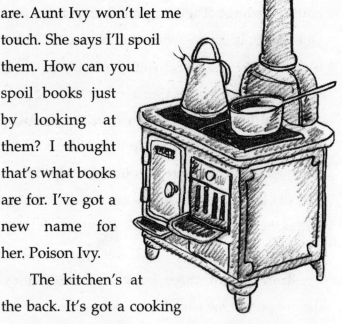

The kitchen's at the back. It's got a cooking range with a fire inside and Uncle Dirt warms his bottom on it. I'm not allowed to. Don't know what's so special about his backside.

❧

Every day's the same here, except Sundays. They make me go to church. I've been four times now. We say prayers and sing hymns, but I don't know the words. Poison Ivy, who is so showy-off about her voice, told me to go la, la, la, and not to sit looking stupid. So I do, and everyone looks at me – as if I'm stupid.

The vicar went on at us for hours today. He said we should think of others before ourselves. I wish Uncle Dirt would do that at dinner time. He stuffs nearly all the potatoes.

When we got home, Stinker nipped my ankle, so I took his bone out in the yard and got rid of it.

There's a little room on the opposite side of the yard from the kitchen, and it's where you pee.

Not in a pot or a bucket like at home! It's called an earth closet, but Poison Ivy calls it the lavatory. In the night, men come on a thing called the violet cart, and they take the muck away. I wouldn't have that job for anything.

The violet cart will have a little extra something to take away next time they call. Stinker's bone.

I'm sick of Uncle Dirt. Every time he walks past, he cuffs me round the ear. He doesn't want me here any more than Poison Ivy does. She says they put up with me because of her poor sister who leads such a dreadful life. What sauce! Ma might be poor, and she might have a hard life, but she's got family who love her. That's more than Poison Ivy has.

I put up with Uncle Dirt and Poison Ivy, but I get my own back every time I go to the lavvy. I make faces at their darling Stinker and throw water at him and call him names. Really rude ones. Yesterday I swear he made a face back at me. He looked just like my aunt.

You could hardly see in front of your nose today. It's a real old London particular, this fog is. I could hardly find the horse when we went to the yard this morning. The fog's a dirty yellow colour – the colour Poison Ivy's face is when she gets up and her hair's all stringy down her neck.

I wish I could go home. Poison Ivy says I'm stupid and I've put the family in danger, and they're better off without me. I hate her. I hate that dog. I hate Uncle Dirt. I've decided to leave. They'll be better off without me, and I'll be better off on my own. At least I won't have to keep on with all that washing business. Waste of time.

I'll do some dipping and nicking and I'll sell

what I steal and pay for lodgings. A room without a bath, that's what I'll get! Won't that be dandy?

I came home filthy from the coal yard and told Poison Ivy I was going upstairs to wash my face before supper. Really I was going to pack my stuff, so I can sneak out early in the morning. But no. Another flipping bath. She's scared I'll 'soil' her bed covers. So what? She doesn't have to sleep in them.

At bedtime, I got everything tied up in one of Poison Ivy's towels. There isn't much. I'm not taking anything of theirs, just the clothes they gave me. And her rotten towel.

Later

It's all gone wrong. I should have gone out the front door, but I couldn't find the key. I got through the kitchen without a sound, and unlocked the back door. Easy. But the moment I set foot in the yard . . .

I'd forgotten the blasted dog. He gave me such a fright I fell into the bucket of potato peelings and cabbage stumps Poison Ivy keeps for someone's pig.

Next second, Uncle Dirt yanked me into the kitchen and gave me such a hiding as I've never had even from Pa. When Poison Ivy realised what was happening, she yelled, 'Oh, my poor sister, who has such a dreadful life! Now her stupid son wants to run away and worry her till she's run ragged!' Then her eyes popped. She looked like a codfish. 'My towel! Bert, he's stealing my towel!'

'Rotten little scab' was the politest thing he called me. I've been in the bedroom ever since. If it wasn't so far down, I'd jump out of the window.

I'm not allowed downstairs except to empty my pot and washstand bowl once a day. I'm surprised they don't make me chuck it out of the window. I'm just glad my room's at the front and I can see what's going on outside.

Yesterday I watched the milk cart go past. The horse is old and bony. It's very slow. So is the milk woman. That gave me an idea.

What if I was to jump out of my window on to the cart? I could be off before the milk woman even noticed. The only danger might be if I timed it wrong and missed. Trott goes splott!

Poison Ivy came up with my supper – bread, cheese and an ancient apple. She looked as if she

was sucking a wasp. While I chewed the bread, I got a brilliant idea. The apple's old and wrinkled, and looks tasteless. But perhaps a horse wouldn't mind a few wrinkles . . .

This morning

I put my plan into action. I opened my window wide, and put on my jacket and cap. I pulled the bed over to the window so I could climb on the sill.

The milk cart turned the corner. As it reached

next door but one on the right, I got ready. My plan was to chuck the apple into the gutter outside next door on the left. When the horse stopped to eat it, the cart would be right beneath my window and I could jump.

I took aim and threw. The apple landed just right. The horse plodded towards it. Had he spotted it? Suddenly, a movement caught my eye. Some horrible shaggy-haired kid had come from nowhere and grabbed my apple!

'Oy!' I shouted. 'Put that back, rat!'

'You chucked it away,' the boy yelled back, and took a bite.

The horse plodded on. The milk churns clanged together as the cart bumped over the cobbles. For a moment I thought I might take a chance and jump anyway, but I heard footsteps, and slammed the window shut. Just in time.

'What is that bed doing over there?' snapped Poison Ivy. 'And what are you doing on it in those filthy shoes?'

I pulled my cuff down over my hand and rubbed the window. 'There was a dirty mark. I was cleaning it,' I said. Quick thinking, Alfie!

She wasn't impressed. 'Hat off indoors,' was all she said, before she locked the door.

I saved my apples, so by this morning I had two. Window up, coat on, ready to go.

The milk cart rattled closer. When the horse was level with next door on the right, I tossed an apple to the left, just as before. But this time, I watched for that shaggy-haired kid.

He had the nerve to look up and grin as he sped across the road. But I was ready.

Wham! The second apple got him right on the nose! That wiped the grin off his face.

The boy yelled and shook his fist at me. I couldn't care less what he did, because the horse stopped. It picked up my apple!

And I jumped.

I've got nowhere to sleep. Every time I find a doorway where I can curl up out of the wind, some bloke comes along and kicks me out. Last night I kept warm for a bit near a roast chestnut man's brazier. Whenever someone walked by, he told me to clear off in case I put them off their grub! Reckon I must look a sight!

I've managed to get just enough to eat these past few days, but that's about it. Today I've had a few chestnuts and a pie.

I wouldn't have had nothing to drink today if I hadn't been such a 'charmer'. That's what the hot coffee seller called me, after I told her she reminded me of a beautiful lady I once saw riding a white horse in Hyde Park. That wasn't exactly true. She actually reminded me of the horse. Anyway, all I got was the dregs from the bottom of her container. It was bitter, but it was wet and warm.

It's going to rain. Soon I'll be wet and cold. I've got to find somewhere to sleep or, at least, to shelter.

I know it's February because I heard someone say, 'Almost windy enough for March.'

Last night I crept down an alley beside an ironmonger's shop. In the yard I found some sacks, so I made myself a soft bed. Well, I thought it was soft till I found something horribly sharp. Yowch! How was I to know ironmongers have their nails delivered in sacks?

It started to rain, but in the corner I found a tin bath, just like Poison Ivy's. This time I didn't get in it – I got under it. At first I thought I'd never sleep with the rain plink-plonking on the bath. But I was so tired, I soon dropped off and slept like a log.

Until . . . a woman found me. I don't know who screamed loudest!

In seconds, a tall, thin man in a black apron had me by the scruff of the neck. He shook me so hard I thought my head would fall off.

But the woman grabbed his arm and said, 'Stop, Joe! Can't you see he's in a bad way? He's soaked!'

Too blooming right, I was. The bath was full of holes.

In minutes, I was in a warm kitchen, clutching a big cup of hot tea. My clothes were draped,

steaming, around the cooking range, and I was wrapped in a cosy blanket. Thought I was in heaven, I did.

'Find out what you can, Jessie,' said the man. 'I've got to open the shop.'

'Let him rest first,' said the woman. She was so kind. She told me they'd had a son my age, but he'd died of a disease called diphtheria.

The ironmonger and his wife let me sleep all morning on a mattress in a tiny room at the back of the house. It was lovely.

That night I found myself telling Mr Penny, the ironmonger, and his wife, all about myself. I told the truth, too. I've never done that before! But the Pennys were so kind, I couldn't help it.

They were upset about me leaving home, and asked if there was any way I could go back. They even offered to speak to Mr Barkitt! But I said it would probably make things worse if they did. Crikey! He'd eat people like them, and not bother to spit the bones out.

At bedtime, I couldn't sleep. Soon I needed to go, but I couldn't find a pot. I crept downstairs, opened the back door and went to the lavvy. When I'd finished, I found Mr Penny in the kitchen doorway.

He must have thought I was going to leg it, because he said, 'Don't run away, lad. If you'll help me in the shop, we'll feed you and keep you safe. You'll never have to steal again.'

I was suspicious. No one's ever been that nice to me before. 'What about Mrs Penny?' I asked.

'It was her idea,' he said, with a sad smile. I

think he was remembering his own boy.

So here I am. One in the eye for old Barkitt, eh? A home and a proper job! Pa would be pleased about the home, but he'd be disgusted about the job.

I know now that it's really Mrs Penny who wants me here. Mr Penny don't trust me. Every night when we close the shop, he frisks me to see if I've nicked anything. He checks my pockets, my shoes, and under my cap. But I haven't stolen anything since I've been here. Why bother? I'm well fed, and Mrs Penny even got me some more clothes. I'm not sure, but they might be brand new.

I went out delivering for Mr Penny this morning as usual. In a narrow street, I saw a woman drop a little package. Nobody noticed, except me. I picked it up and slipped into an alley.

I ducked behind a crate and was picking at the knotted string when a voice whispered. 'You nicked that, then?'

It was a short, scruffy kid.

'Course I did,' I said. I don't know why I lied. It's just that the kid looked at me with big, wide eyes, and it made me feel important. Anyway, it was a sort of nicking.

I unwrapped the parcel. When I saw what was inside, I threw it down in disgust. Cheese!

The kid gawped at me. He stared at the cheese, lying in the dirt, then back at me. 'D-don't you want it?'

'No.' I was still full of breakfast. 'You have it.'

The kid couldn't have had a proper meal in weeks. I remember feeling like that. I don't know where he'd been. His clothes were stiff with what looked like mud. At least, I hope it was mud. It stank something terrible.

The air smelled fresh today. Mrs Penny said she had her special spring feeling. 'It happens every year,' she said. 'You wake up one morning, and you know spring's arrived.' I've never noticed it before, but she's right.

It was so nice that after I'd done my deliveries, I decided to go down to the river instead of going straight back. It's pongy there, but there's always plenty to watch. The water was low, and the shore was littered with mudlarks.

Trudging through deep mud looking for things to sell can't be such a bad job on a lovely day like this, but I bet it's even stinkier in the summer.

Suddenly, someone shouted, 'Hey!' I turned to run, then realised there was no need. I'd done nothing wrong. Well, not since the cheese, and that turned out OK in the end, because it fed the kid.

And blow me down, there *was* the kid! He scrambled up the bank towards me. He was a mudlark! No wonder he stank. His little basket was full of wet, muddy coal.

'Hello,' he said. 'Nicked anything good lately?'

'Loads,' I lied. 'I'm a trained pickpocket.'

He put his hands over his pockets.

'Don't worry,' I said. 'I don't nick from friends.'

He laughed, and we chatted for a bit. He told me he'll get twopence for his coal. 'Not a bad morning,' he said. His name's Timmy.

Late this afternoon, I delivered an oil lamp to a posh house, and it was getting dark by the time I turned back. Next thing, who should I bump into but Timmy again. His pockets bulged, and the front of his coat was stuffed with I-don't-know-what, and his basket was full. He told me he was off home. I said if it wasn't far I'd give him a hand.

He took me down a dirty little alley. There were broken-down doors here and there, and

windows so filthy you couldn't see through them. We trod through piles of rotting rubbish and turned left at the end by a deep ditch.

Timmy lives through a broken door at the end of a wall. Kids there have lots of space to play, but it must be dangerous. Suppose they fall in that ditch? It only needs one sniff to tell you what goes in there – nobody would want to drown in that!

Timmy kicked the door open and took me inside. The house stank. The stairs were rotten, and he told me to put my feet exactly where he did. We went up three narrow flights and came to a tiny landing. Timmy stopped by a door and started to unload his day's pickings.

I jerked my head towards the door. 'Ain't we going in?' I asked.

He shook his head. 'Old Ma Flanagan lives in there,' he explained. 'I sleep out here.' He must have seen my face, because he went on hurriedly, 'Oh, I've got a bed, but it stays in Ma Flanagan's room during the day, so it don't get nicked.'

Just then, there was a wheezing, puffing

sound, and a steady thumping that got nearer and nearer. Timmy's face lit up. 'It's Ma Flanagan!'

'Hello, Timmy, love,' said Ma Flanagan. 'Had a good day today, I did. Got a nice bit of fish for our supper.'

I could see that. The fish was looking at me from the top of her shawl.

Ma Flanagan stared. 'Who are you?'

'I'm, er – going,' I said, and took off down the stairs before she invited me to supper.

'Bye then, Going,' she cackled.

I went downstairs a bit too fast. I took the last flight in one go and nearly bashed my brains out on what was left of the front door.

I saw Timmy on and off over the next week. He told me Ma Flanagan's not his mother. That's just what people call her. She lets him sleep on her landing so she can keep an eye on him, she says. But Timmy reckons he keeps an eye on her. She hasn't got much, but she shares with him, and if he finds anything good, he shares with her. Most mudlarks work alone, but Timmy stays near Ma, and sometimes slips something in her basket to help out. Her back must ache, bent over like that for hours.

Timmy wanted to know about me. I told him I was on the run from the peelers. He wasn't half impressed. I said I was a big-time pickpocket in my own part of town, and couldn't go back till the manhunt was off. He asked me to teach him to thieve, but I said I don't do much nicking at the moment – I'm pretending to be a normal person with a job and that.

Yesterday he asked, 'Can I see where you work?' I said, 'OK, but don't let yourself be seen with me, or you might get arrested.' That gave him the shivers, I could see, but he thought it was exciting!

I took him to the corner by Mr Groom the saddler's, and showed him our shop.

'There's a lot of stuff,' Timmy said. 'Don't you ever nick anything?'

I shook my head. I couldn't have even if I'd wanted to, because of Mr Penny frisking me every night. But with a friend like Timmy on the outside . . .

I shoved those thoughts right out of my bonce.

Church today. It's all right, going with the Pennys. Their vicar doesn't shout like Poison Ivy's. I know some of the hymns now – they sing the same ones over and over, so you can't help picking them up. I like a good singsong, I do.

The rest of today was my own, so I went to the river. I knew the mudlarks would be working, even on Sunday. So were the toshers. I didn't want to go near them though – they poke about near the sewers, where even the mudlarks won't go. It makes my stomach heave just thinking about it.

I spotted Timmy and yelled. He waved for me to go down on to the shore. I whipped off my shoes and rolled up my trousers. The sludge squidged horribly between my toes. Ugh.

Timmy was helping Ma Flanagan. Her collecting basket's got a huge hole in it and the handle's nearly split through. Yesterday she lost a lovely little spoon, he said, and some coal and good nails. Now she has to carry her finds in her skirt.

'You need two hands to feel for stuff,' said Timmy. 'And you must be quick, in case someone else gets there first.'

I felt sorry for Ma Flanagan, so I helped, too. When we took the stuff back to her room, she invited me to stay for a bite to eat. With Ma Flanagan, it's not so much invite, as order.

We had eels and bread. I tried not to look at

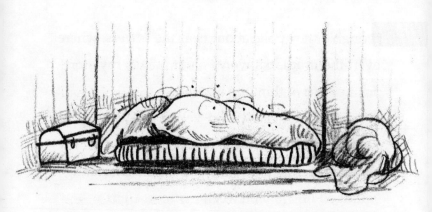

Ma Flanagan's bed – it was covered with fleas. No
wonder she's always scratching. Timmy's bed,
that he takes out at night, was just a bundle of
rags in the corner.

I did something yesterday I didn't expect to do. It
began when we opened up. I put the stuff out as
usual.

I hung a big basket on a hook beside the front
window.

I thought about that basket all day. At five
o'clock, Mr Penny gave me two saws and a ham-
mer to deliver to the theatre. 'Ask round the back
for the head carpenter,' he said. 'Don't go near the

front doors.'

Mrs Penny called us for some cake. I shoved mine in my pocket and picked up the tools. As I went out I looked back. Mr Penny was tucking in and talking away. I reached up, lifted the basket down and hurried off to the theatre.

A posh man came out of the theatre and dropped his ticket. One day I'll buy one and go through the front door like him. The doorman will call me 'sir'.

The theatre doorman asked me what I was hanging about for. He didn't call me 'sir', though, he called me 'you young urchin'.

'I've got some tools for the carpenter,' I said. He looked at what I was carrying. 'Oh, and a basket,' I added.

'What does he want a woman's basket for?' asked the man.

'Keep his knick-knacks in?' I suggested.

'Don't give me lip,' said the man. 'Round the back. Stage door.'

It wasn't as grand round the back! It was weird. There were men with make-up on, and ladies with very fancy outfits and their legs showing! Music and singing, too. I'd like to have stayed but I had something special to do. I got shot of the tools and headed for the river.

The water was getting high, so Timmy and Ma Flanagan were quite near. 'Hey!' I yelled. They waved, but carried on working. I kept yelling till Timmy trudged over to see what I wanted. I gave him the basket, and whispered in his ear (it was filthy). His eyes lit up. He ran to Ma

Flanagan and thrust a handle at her. She took it, and listened to him. Then she slowly straightened her stiff back and turned to look at me. I'll never forget her face. It made me come over all warm. And happy.

I felt a bit bad about the basket, but I told myself it didn't hurt Mr Penny. He's got loads more. He didn't notice it was missing, because I made sure it was me who brought in all the stuff that night. Next morning, I put another basket outside.

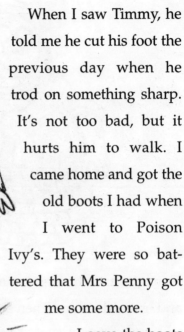

When I saw Timmy, he told me he cut his foot the previous day when he trod on something sharp. It's not too bad, but it hurts him to walk. I came home and got the old boots I had when I went to Poison Ivy's. They were so battered that Mrs Penny got me some more.

I gave the boots to Timmy. They won't keep the wet out, but he can wear them going to and from the river. They're so big he keeps walking out of them!

I delivered a mended boot scraper to a man in the Strand this afternoon. That's near the river, so I went down to watch the boats. Mrs Penny had

given me a slice of apple pie, wrapped in a cloth, so I ate it in the sun, watching everyone else working.

A woman peeling shrimps called, 'Penny for 'em, love?' For a minute I thought she meant the shrimps, but she didn't. She wanted to know my thoughts.

'I was thinking that one day I'll sail away to a far country,' I said, 'on a beautiful steamship – and I'll travel first class. And see wonderful things.'

She snorted. 'That's what my old man did,'

she said. 'Only it wasn't first class he went, and the only wonderful things he saw were kangy roos or whatever they have in Australia.'

I shivered. 'What did he do?'

'Burglar. Good one, too.'

Not that good, or he wouldn't have been nicked and transported to Australia. But some people say there's gold to be had there. You just have to dig it up. I think Australia would be exciting. Like an adventure.

Bit of luck yesterday! The road was too mucky to cross, even for me, and I wasn't paying a crossing sweeper when I could move to a clearer part.

I was about to shift, when a hansom cab pulled up just past me. Suddenly, the horse whinnied and jumped, and the cab rolled backwards. When the wheel touched my shoulder, I leaped aside. Then I had a brainwave.

I banged on the bit where the driver's feet go, and yelled, 'Ow! My foot!'

The driver was struggling with the reins, but a passenger poked his head out, saw me and told him, 'Stop, you fool!' Actually, he was ruder than that.

The man got out, followed by a lady. He brushed me down, and asked if I was all right. 'Just a bruise, guv,' I said, limping around in a circle. 'See? I can still walk. Ooooh,' I groaned.

'Poor boy,' said the lady. 'Give him something, George, darling.'

George darling gave me a shilling!

As the hansom cab trick worked so well, I tried it again today. I put Timmy by the wheel, then I shouted at someone on the other side of the street – right into the horse's ear!

It all went wrong. Timmy bellowed so loud I realised the wheel really had gone over his foot. The passenger – a great big woman with too much make-up – told him to 'clear orf'. No shilling that time.

I thought there'd be a horrible mess of bone and blood in Timmy's boot, but the wheel missed his toes completely and just ran over empty boot.

I was sweeping up this morning after the butcher had trodden sawdust all over the floor, when I spotted something shiny. A silver sixpence!

I was about to give it to Mr Penny when Timmy peered round the corner of the window.

'Get rid of that young guttersnipe before he makes off with something, Alfie,' said Mr Penny.

Blimey! It wasn't long ago that people had been calling me a guttersnipe. Now I'm chasing them away. I have come up in the world!

I went outside. 'Mr Penny says push off,' I said loudly, then whispered, 'Wotcher doing 'ere?'

'Brought you this,' said Timmy, holding out a smooth stone, shaped like a boot. 'It's for luck,' he said, "cos you gave me these.' He looked down proudly at his boots.

The silver sixpence was still in my hand. I

shoved it at Timmy and said, 'Get something nice for Ma Flanagan's supper.' Then I shouted, 'And don't come back!'

Mr Penny was pleased. He said, 'Well done, lad.'

I don't suppose the sixpence was his, anyway.

I've noticed Mr Penny leaves his till open sometimes. It sticks, and he's worried he'll break it if he keeps bashing it shut. 'Must fix that,' he keeps saying.

The till's full of coins. Mr Penny can't need all of them. He wouldn't miss a few. Just one or two. And wouldn't a couple of coins here and there help Timmy and old Ma Flanagan! Yesterday, I slipped a shilling into my pocket. I'd told Timmy to come and hang about outside as soon as he could, and I'd pass it to him.

I waited all day. Eventually Mr Penny rammed the till shut. It was near closing time. I had to get rid of the shilling before he frisked me!

What a relief when I saw Timmy's dirty little face. 'There's that young guttersnipe, Mr Penny,' I yelled. 'I'll chase him away!' I ran outside and Timmy darted off. Not far, though. He stopped outside Mr Groom's shop and waited. I shoved the shilling in his hand. He gaped at it. I had to put one hand on his head and the other under his chin to shut his jaw!

'Blimey!' he said. 'Ma will be so happy. She's poorly. She can't work, Alfie.'

'I'll get some more tomorrow,' I said. Mr Penny won't notice.

83

I gave Timmy sixpence today. I can't take more than one coin at a time because they'd jingle in my pocket. But I did manage to swipe a good strong candle holder off the shop front. That'll be useful for Ma Flanagan. Or she could pawn it.

Later Timmy brought a message from Ma Flanagan. She says I'm a good soul, and will go to heaven. Not yet, I hope!

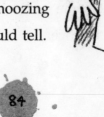

I delivered a coal vase to a house today. Vase? Fancy name for a box, if you ask me.

The cook was snoozing when I knocked, I could tell.

One side of her hair was all scruffy, and she had dribble in the corner of her mouth.

'The family's away,' said the cook, 'so you can take it up to the nursery yourself.'

I headed for the stairs. 'Wait, lad,' she said. 'Fill the vase up first. It'll save the housemaid's legs.'

Flipping cheek! What about my legs? I was about to ask what I should fill it up with – roses? – when I caught her eye and decided not to push my luck. I loaded it with coal and carried it up three flights of stairs. Never took her eyes off me, she didn't, and I ain't surprised. The stuff they had in that house! A burglar could live off it for the rest of his life.

The nursery was something else. How come a couple of kids have all that, and others, like my brothers and sisters, are scrunched up in a tiny, dingy room? It's not fair.

When I got back, Mr Groom was talking to Mr Penny. I didn't like the way he looked at me. Mr Penny's clattered round for days, counting things and writing in a book. Stocktaking, he says.

He wants to be sure of what he's got, so he can tell if anything goes missing.

He's mended the till.

This morning I was eating bread and dripping when Mr Penny said, 'While you were out yesterday, Alfie, that young guttersnipe was snooping round.'

'Don't worry, Mr Penny,' I said. 'I'll chase him off next time.'

'I don't think there'll be a next time,' he said.

'Mr Groom caught him, and I took a stick to him. If he comes round again, I'll hand him to the police.'

I heard of a kid that was hanged for stealing a pair of boots. I couldn't bear to think of Timmy . . .

I swallowed. 'D'you think he's a bad 'un, then?'

'Somebody's been stealing from me,' said Mr Penny. 'It's not Mrs Penny. And it couldn't be you, could it, Alfie?'

Flip! The way he looked at me! I shook my head so hard my ears flapped. 'No, sir,' I said. 'I bet it's that young guttersnipe!'

I haven't been near Timmy for a week, and he hasn't been near the shop. I hope he's OK.

Yesterday I worked so hard packing up nails in seven pound parcels that Mr Penny said I can have a half day off today. And it's not even Christmas!

I spent the afternoon at the river. Timmy's

OK, but Ma Flanagan's really poorly. 'She hardly eats,' he told me. I helped him collect for a bit, then I remembered what Mr Penny had said. 'Did he hurt you?' I asked.

Timmy rubbed his bottom, remembering. 'No,' he lied.

Mr Penny watches me like a blackbird watching a spider nowadays. He always shuts the till, and he frisks me at odd times, as if he's trying to catch me out. I'm fed up with it. He obviously doesn't trust me any more. I don't know why I don't go back to my original plan of being a pickpocket. A great pickpocket.

I'd better get practising.

I actually got a woman's purse yesterday! She was so busy looking at stupid frilly hats that she didn't even notice me. Timmy was dead impressed. I decided to train him to work with me. I can pass things to him, like Pa used to do to me. It'll be less dangerous.

Had a near thing today when I tried to dip someone who was getting in a carriage. The driver turned, saw me and shouted to the passenger, 'Look out behind you!'

'Leg it!' I yelled to Timmy. Some look-out he turned out to be. Now he's got the nerve to keep having a go at me! I told him I'm out of practice, but he reckons I never was a pickpocket. 'I am!' I yelled at the top of my voice. 'I'm the son of the best pickpocket in London!'

That was stupid.

Timmy sneered. 'Your dad's never a pick

pocket,' he said. 'Bet you haven't even got a dad. You're a norphan like me.'

That did it! I thumped him. I'll show him.

Just one week back picking pockets, and I got nicked! I can't believe it, but I did. I was on my own in a busy street, traffic everywhere, and crowds walking, shopping and watching the musicians.

A woman took her purse out, paid for a blue ribbon, and dropped the purse and ribbon into her maid's basket. Then she went to look at the puppy-seller. The maid followed. So did I. They were asking for it. I stood behind them and whipped the ribbon and the purse.

Next minute my legs were kicking air.

Everything happened so fast. One minute the crowd was shouting at

me and pointing, the next I was in the police station, and the next I was up before the beak.

'Call the magistrate "Your Honour",' they said. Magistrate, beak, Your Honour, m'lud – it's all the same. They punish you.

I was lucky, the beak said. Lucky not to be hanged. Lucky not to be transported to Australia.

'Oh, lor!' I thought. 'It's the birch.'

But it wasn't. He sent me to prison for twenty-one days' hard labour. 'Thank you, m'lud,' I said. I was so relieved.

I always thought hard labour would be smashing huge chunks of stone with giant hammers, but it can be all sorts of things. Some prisoners here make sacks, do ironwork or carpentry, make brushes, or even knit. It's odd seeing grown men with knitting needles, swearing over their dropped stitches!

What makes the labour so hard is that we do it all day with hardly a break. We can't talk (unless we want to be thumped by a warder), and we don't get enough to eat. I'm always hungry.

I've got a sitting-down job. I have to pick oakum. And I truly hope I don't have to do this for the whole three weeks.

I get a piece of tarry rope, and I have to pull the fibres apart – they're the oakum. Because the rope's all gummed up with thick black tar, the fibres are stuck together, so it's really hard. It's deadly work and my hands are already so sore they bleed. I keep thinking of people in the work-house who have to pick oakum all the time. Poor souls.

I'm so cold. I don't think I've ever been so cold. That's one of the worst things about prison. The cold gets right into my bones, like toothache in my arms and legs. I was cold when I went to bed yesterday, cold every time I woke in the night, and still cold when I woke this morning.

The only time I warmed up was when we were allowed out for some fresh air in a yard, for exercise. Some exercise! The yard's so small that if you walked too fast you'd smack into the opposite wall in two seconds – that's if you don't bounce off someone else going in the opposite direction first.

Some people in here have got money, or friends on the outside. They can afford to have food sent in. I haven't got a penny. I haven't even got a friend. I have to eat what I'm given. At least the meals break up the day. But dinner today was just the most horrible, disgusting thing I've had in here – even worse than usual. It was two small, hard potatoes floating in thin, greasy liquid, with a great lump of bacon fat. I couldn't cut it into little bits, because we aren't allowed knives, only spoons. I had trouble swallowing that slimy fat without being sick. And you'd think you'd be safe with potatoes, but no. Most of them were rotten inside. Now I don't feel very well.

Yesterday was mostly horrible. I found a cockroach in my soup. I'm not surprised. Those disgusting bedbug-eating creatures are everywhere – I'm forever hearing them scuttling about in the night, or clattering to the floor when they drop off the walls. Ugh.

Anyway, as I said, the day was mostly horrible, but something nice happened. I met a man called Sid. 'Sid the Star-glazer', he called himself. When he heard my name, he said, 'Dan Trott's nipper?' Sid saw my pa only three weeks ago. He told me Pa and Ma worry about what's happened to me. That made me happy, and sad, as well. When I went to bed, I cried. But no one heard. No one cares.

Today Sid asked what I'm going to do when I get out. 'Dunno,' I said. 'I can't go back. Mr Barkitt's out for my blood.'

Sid shuddered. 'He runs that whole district,' he said. 'Best stay away. Everyone fears Barkitt.' Then he gave me a good tip.

'If you ever want to sell anything,' he said, 'go to my brother, Fred the dolly man. Say Sid sent you. He'll deal with you straight.'

A dolly shop is like a pawnbroker's, but it's not exactly lawful. It's where people take stuff they nicked. They can sell it to the dolly man, or pawn it. I'll remember about Fred.

Even though I see Sid sometimes, I'm so lonely. It's dreadful. I'm scared all the time. There are

97

some horrible people in here. Some of them are real mean old lags. One man's got a knife and he keeps threatening people with it, even if they're only looking at him. He's supposed to have cut someone's ear off once. I don't look at anybody except Sid. If it wasn't for him, I don't know how I'd get through this. He even made me laugh today! And he's teaching me useful things. He's already explained how to open a window quietly, and how star-glazers work. Today he told me the best way to steal clothes.

Two of you wait for a laundry cart to collect washing from a posh house. Once the baskets are loaded up they're tied on with cord. Follow the cart to a quiet street. Then one of you gets hold of a basket, while the other cuts the cord. Now carry it away, all neat and tidy-like! Can't wait to try this!

I asked Sid what he's going to do when he gets out.

'Well, lad,' he said, 'I'd like to tell you as I'm going to lead a straight and honest life. That's what I've always told meself before, every time I've been put away for a stretch.' Sid's been inside a few times.

'I'll try to get work,' he went on, 'but I know what'll happen. I reckon as people can almost smell the prison on me – no one will give me a chance. So what'll I do?'

'Steal something?' I said.

Sid nodded. 'It's not easy to be honest, young Alfie,' he said. 'You'll see.'

Nothing's easy here, but night's just the worst. I lie here, imagining the cockroaches feeding on the bedbugs, the bedbugs feeding on the lice, the lice feeding on the fleas, and the fleas feeding on me. I don't think I've got an inch of skin that hasn't been bitten. But it's no good complaining. It doesn't matter how miserable and cold I get, I'll never complain. If you do, you get a doing – that means a warder beats you up. It's hard enough staying on the right side of the prisoners.

The most important thing Sid drummed into me was just to get on with my oakum, keep my head down and stay away from trouble. 'You'll be out before you know it,' he said. And that's what got me through these past three weeks, because now I am out. But what now, I wondered?

All I had to sleep in last night was a broken crate stuffed with straw.

It's so good to be free. I don't ever want to go

inside again. Maybe, I thought, I should forget thieving. Yes. I decided. I was never going to steal again, and I was going straight back to work at Mr Penny's. There was nowhere else to go.

On the way, I planned how I'd say sorry, and how I'd convince Mr and Mrs Penny that I've changed my ways. Then I'd beg for another chance.

I nearly cried when I saw the shop was shut. I ran into Mr Groom's and asked what was wrong. He said Mr Penny's had bad chest trouble, and he's been so ill that he and Mrs Penny had to shut the shop up. They've gone to stay in Brighton, with Mrs Penny's brother, for the good sea air.

Mr Groom was huffy with me. I knew why. 'I'm not really bad,' I said. 'I came back to say sorry.' I sniffed. He looked at me, then jerked his head towards the back of the shop. 'There's bread and cheese there. It'll keep you going. And keep your thieving hands to yourself.'

There was a lot of stuff at the back of his shop. There was even a set of boots for a horse to wear while it's pulling a lawn-mower! Whatever next? A sunhat?

While I ate, Mr Groom told me Mr Penny kept saying he must be going off his nut, because things were missing when he knew they couldn't possibly be. I know why Mr Groom said that. I

went scarlet – I could feel it. I was too ashamed to hang around, and left as soon as I'd finished eating. I didn't take anything.

Today, I stood outside the Ragged School. They feed you there and it's warm. I'd feel odd in school, though. I'm a working man, I am. But I was that hungry I nearly went in. Luckily, I saw someone hadn't finished their ginger beer, and the stallholder let me have it. She gave me a sausage as well, that was too burnt for her to eat – she was a bit short on teeth and if she broke any more, she said, she'd have to go to the surgeon. 'I'm not going through that agony,' she grumbled. 'I wish doctors could make you go to sleep when they do things to you.' Hah! Some hopes!

I decided to find Timmy. Perhaps Ma Flanagan will let me share his landing.

Timmy was thrilled to see me, and kept touching my arm. He wanted to know what prison was like. I didn't want to talk about it. 'Where's Ma Flanagan?' I asked.

'She's dead,' he said. I touched his arm then. He turned away, and when he looked back, his eyes were watery.

'Where d'you sleep?' I asked.

'Under the bridge,' he said. 'It's cold at night, Alfie.'

Tonight I brought Timmy to the market, and found him some straw and a box. He had enough money for hot coffee, and I found some split tomatoes that had been thrown away.

It's got to be better than this. And I'm going to make it better for me and Timmy. But I won't forget that I stole from Mr Penny, who was really kind to me. He didn't deserve it. I won't hurt people any more. I'll have to steal again, though. Just for now.

See? One day I promise myself I'm not going to steal any more, another day I decide I've got to. And that's the trouble. There ain't a lot of choice for the likes of me. If you're too scruffy and dirty, or too young, and if you're not good at anything, you have to get your dinner the best way you can. If there were more people like Mr Penny, who'd give a chance to a poor kid, maybe it would be different. But, like Sid said, it's hard to be honest. Much easier to nick a pie.

Yesterday, I did my first break-in, at the house with the flash nursery. Timmy kept watch, and I went down into the area and opened the pantry window. I did it how Sid told me, and it worked.

There was a little safe, where they put food to keep the flies off. I found a lovely meat pie, some butter and cold roast beef!

I could hear the cook shouting at someone, so I had to be quick. A silver dish full of sweetmeats sat on the table. They were lovely. I scoffed the lot before I got back to Timmy. We found a little park and hid in some bushes to eat our picnic. Timmy scooped up all the butter with his half of the pie, and then we polished off the beef. I felt a bit sick afterwards. Timmy was sick.

There was still the sweetmeat dish! We took it to Sid's brother, Fred the dolly man. He was so glad to hear from someone who'd seen Sid that he took us out the back and gave us milk and rhubarb pie!

Fred said any friend of Sid's was a friend of his. 'I'll give you best prices for anything you, er, find,' he said.

He bought the dish, and Timmy and I left with enough cash to pay for food and lodgings for quite a while. Last night, we slept like toffs. Only two to a bed and it was big enough for us to sleep side by side.

The dinner was greasy, but warm, and it doesn't take much to fill my tum these days.

Just last night, I told Timmy that if ever he was collared by a peeler, he was to drop to the ground and scream 'Let me go!'

Blow me down, today, when he was nicking a couple of oranges for a snack, the greengrocer caught him. Timmy flung the oranges away, then started screaming and yelling and kicking.

The women shouted things at the man like, 'Shame!' and 'Pick on someone your own size!' and 'He's starving, poor thing!'

The man let Timmy go. He didn't want his customers to think he was cruel. I've seen this work before, but I've never tried it myself.

We're doing really well, me and Timmy, pinching things from basement areas. We never steal from poor people, though. We're like that man in the olden days, Robbing Hood or something.

But I keep thinking that Ma and Pa would want me to be better than this. A pickpocket like Pa is respected, but no one thinks much of an area sneak.

We've tried a few other things, Timmy and me. The laundry cart trick worked a treat, till I realised the poor laundry woman would get blamed for losing the clothes, or even accused of stealing them. We won't do that again.

Everything Timmy and I 'find' we take to Fred. He gives me good prices. I think Timmy and I should try to get better lodgings. Perhaps with a bed each. Wouldn't we be grand!

Timmy and I have got what we've been dreaming

of! Our new room's in the same lodging house, so there are still fleas and stuff, but we've got a little bed each, in a tiny room, and we're dry and comfortable. If we shut the door and open the window, we can hardly smell the rest of the house.

Poison Ivy had a cupboard nearly as big as our room, but I'd rather be here any day.

Last night, as it was getting dark, we saw a man and kid leaning against a sweetshop window. They looked innocent enough, but I reckoned they were up to something.

I saw the man fiddle about at a small window-pane, then the kid reached inside and grabbed a couple of handfuls of sweets. No one else noticed, but I knew what they were doing.

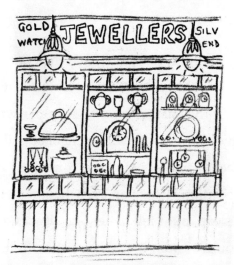

Star-glazing! I remembered Sid telling me how to do it. Well, if it was that easy . . . !

I took Timmy up to Oxford Street, where there are really nice shops. We hung about opposite a jeweller's. We had to wait until the owner put the gas lamps out.

When the shop was shut up for the night, we went across and worked in the shadows. Timmy kept watch, and I did exactly what Sid said. First I dug the point of my knife in the corner of a little window pane. The glass cracked in a sort of star pattern. I stuck the knife into the cracked glass and twisted it. The glass splintered, but there was scarcely a sound. Good old Sid! I took out enough glass so I could get my arm in. It was easy! Mind you, I got the shakes good and proper when we got home. Suppose we'd been nabbed – it would have been more than the birch, I reckon. Transportation, I bet, or even hanging! I could hardly sleep, but I felt better once it was daylight and I could be sure we'd got away with it.

I feel better still now I've had a good chance to look at the loot! We didn't take all that much stuff – just enough to make sure life gets better for us.

And I've got a plan.

Later

Fred was staggered at what we'd got. He can't pay for it all at once, but I trust him to give us some each day until he's paid for it.

Mind, I didn't give him all the things we took. I kept some stuff back – just small things, that I can hide easily.

Fred said he could use me, if I'd be willing. What he wants is for some of his special customers to bring things they want to sell to me, instead of him.

The peelers get suspicious when there are too many comings and goings at his shop. Then Fred will come to my lodging house and collect the

things, and he'll pay me. Then I pay his special customers, only I keep some of the money for myself. That's how it works.

Tonight, me and Timmy have got a room each to sleep in. It's in a fine house, where we get a good meat dinner with gravy.

I can't believe it. Two weeks, and I'm making all this money, and I don't do any work for it. I don't have to go thieving or anything. Nor does Timmy. I know what I do isn't what you'd call honest, but I don't feel I'm a thief exactly. It's more like I'm a businessman – buying and selling, and suchlike.

I gave a penny to the organ grinder's monkey

this evening, then Timmy gave some to a blind beggar. The beggar said, 'Bless you, sir.' Timmy liked that.

It's nice giving money to people who haven't got it. In the market we found some of the kids who sleep on roofs. I gave one threepence and he ran and showed his friends. 'Thanks, mister,' they called. Mister! I'm going to give pennies away more often. Not too many, mind.

Tomorrow, I'm going to disguise myself and go and see Ma and Pa, because I've got presents for them. Didn't I promise myself I'd change our lives? Well, I've changed mine, no question, and these presents will change theirs. Won't I be proud!

❦ ❦ ❦

This morning, I took the stuff I kept from when we robbed the jewellers, tucked it inside my shirt and headed back to my old home. I couldn't risk being recognised by Mr Barkitt or Ginger, so I borrowed some things from Fred's shop, and dressed up as a butcher's boy. As I got near, I kept my hat down low over my eyes, and stared into my basket.

I hoped nobody would ask me for sausages. The only things under that cloth were dirty clothes.

I was walking by a little park, when everything went quiet, except for the rumble of wheels. I glanced up. It

was a funeral procession.

I took my hat off, because that's respectful when you see a funeral. Big mistake. When I stuck it back on, I put my head down, turned and walked – smack – into a great fat belly. I squinted up and nearly passed out when I saw ginger side-whiskers.

'I'll be jiggered! It's Trott!' roared Ginger.

'I – I'm not thieving,' I protested. 'I just want to see Ma and Pa.'

Ginger laughed – not a funny laugh. 'You're going nowhere . . .' he began. But I was! I scarpered, round the corner, up the street and into the alley where our old house is. I banged on the door. An old lady I'd never seen before stuck her head out.

'Trotts?' I said.

'Gorn,' she whispered. 'Mr Barkitt said they couldn't live here no more. Go away. I don't want to be seen with you.'

Nobody wanted me.

There was only one other place to look. Poison Ivy's. Sure enough, I found Ma there, with the two youngest. 'Where's Pa and Billy and the others?' I gasped when she finally let me go.

Poison Ivy sniffed. 'Not here, that's for sure. My Bert says . . .'

I couldn't care less what her Bert says. Ma told me Pa and the older kids were up at St Giles's.

I said, 'Wait here. Pa will be back for you, I promise.' She burst into tears.

Early yesterday, I headed for St Giles's. I know all about it – the biggest rookery in London. I was scared I'd get lost in all the alleys and yards. It's a dangerous place to get lost in. I suppose it's called a rookery because it's crowded and noisy like where rooks live in the treetops. I know where I'd rather be. Tweet, tweet!

I walked into a yard full of people. The second they saw me, they froze. They didn't look friendly. The kids jumped up and vanished, like flies do when you kick a rotting bone.

'Trott,' I said. 'I'm Alfie Trott, and I'm looking for my pa.'

A kid bobbed up from behind a heap of something nasty and said, 'You Billy Trott's brother?'

A lump came in my throat. 'D'you know where he is?' I asked.

The kid took me to a window at the base of a wall, slithered through and told me to follow. I climbed after him and dropped down into a filthy cellar. There didn't seem to be any air down there, and it reeked of dirty bodies. There were sacks on the floor, with people asleep on them, and a few rats that took no notice of us at all.

'Is Billy in here?' I whispered.

'Four houses along,' said the kid, and disappeared through a hole in the wall.

I followed him through more holes in walls,

until suddenly there was my little brother.

When Billy saw me, he cried. I didn't. He said I did, but I didn't. Then word must have got round, because all of a sudden there was Pa and all the others.

Pa said I looked a fine young gent! I told him where I live, and that I'd got two good rooms, and he said I've done really well for myself. Then I gave him my presents – rings and earrings and stuff.

'Sell them,' I said. 'Fetch Ma and the little ones and find some lodgings.' His face! Alfie telling Pa what to do! But he listened. 'Then send someone to tell me where you live,' I went on.

'Come back and live with us, Alfie,' Billy begged.

I shook my head. Now I'm back in touch with my family, I can see them often – but I can still have my good life, with a whole bed to myself, and I can do what I want. 'You'll have more room without me,' I said, 'but I'll visit you often.'

It was a lovely day.

Last night, Timmy and I dressed up to go down to the pleasure gardens to celebrate. We saw a tightrope walker and had a go at the shooting gallery, and there were fireworks. I crossed the fortune teller's palm with silver. She told me I'll marry a proper lady and be a rich and famous gent. I will, too.

This afternoon, we were dozing when we

heard a commotion outside. Timmy went to the window. 'There's a cart in the street,' he said, 'with hundreds of people on it – well, about ten . . .'

'Nothing to do with us, Timmy boy,' I said.

But it was. Seconds later, there was a thumping on the stairs, and the landlady called, 'Mr Trott, people to see you.'

Suddenly a voice I knew boomed, 'Out of me way, missis! Let me see my boy!'

In came Pa. In came Ma. In came Billy. In came the whole family, one after the other.

Each was carrying a box or paper parcel. I had a horrible feeling I knew what this meant.

They've been here three days. All my peace and space has gone. But there are good things. Ma doesn't look worried now. Pa's polite to me, and treats me with respect. After all, I'm the one who earns the money.

We've had to rent an extra room, but we all eat together, and talk, and laugh a lot.

Timmy's still here. At least this time they noticed there was an extra one. Everyone likes him. He's just part of our family.

As I said, they've been here three days now. And I love it.

Tonight I did something I've wanted to do for a long time. I went back to the shop.

I was glad to see lights. Mr and Mrs Penny are back. I hope he's well.

I slipped down the alley, where I went that cold rainy night, and there was the old tin bath. Carefully, quietly, I laid it down on the ground exactly where it was the night I slept under it. Then I slipped a pile of coins inside. It was the amount I took for Timmy, plus some extra for the basket I stole for Ma Flanagan.

Mr and Mrs Penny knew I was a thief, but they gave me a chance – treated me like family – and I let them down. OK, I'm not exactly honest and straightforward now, but I try to help people when I can, and I don't hurt anyone who has less than me.

And now that I have my own family back, I've got a lot. I'm happy. Best of all was what Pa

said. 'Life's good for us all, now, Alfie – thanks to you.' I got such a lump in my throat I could hardly swallow.

I'm Mister Alfie Trott, who changed things for his family.

Toby sat up. There were tears in his eyes. 'Why am I crying?' he wondered, once he'd worked out where he was. 'I'm me again, Toby Tucker. I'm not a thief, so I'm miles better off than Alfie.'

And then he remembered Alfie's family, and his eyes prickled. He got up, cross with himself, and ran downstairs. The washing machine was still going and the dogs wanted to play.

Toby went out and sat on the grass. Snowball climbed into his lap, and Barney leaned against him. He heard car doors slam, but stayed where he was, just thinking.

A few minutes later, Don and Evie came into the garden. Don crouched down. 'What's up, lad?'

Toby blinked hard. 'Everyone's going away, and it's all family, family, family. They've all got family.'

Evie sat on the grass beside him. 'Toby, you've got us. And you've got all my family, and Don's family, too.'

Toby picked at a knot in Snowball's coat. 'But they're not *my* family, are they?'

'You don't have to be real family to love someone,' said Evie.

Toby remembered Timmy. Alfie changed things for his family, but he changed things for Timmy, too.

He stood up. 'Don, Evie. Come upstairs. I want to show you something.'

In his room, Toby found the scraps of paper with Alfie's name on them, joined them with sticky tape, and stuck it on his pinboard.

'You found another one!' Don said, delighted.

Toby felt that perhaps, while they were listening to him – really listening – this was the moment to tell them the truth about the chest. 'I did more than find it,' he began, but there was a noise from downstairs. Footsteps, clanging, giggling.

'Hello?' came a voice. 'We're coming up!'

Toby looked at Don and Evie. 'Not in here!' he begged.

But he was too late. Jake and Amber burst into the room with a bucket, three scrapers and a bottle labelled 'Wallpaper Stripper'.

'Here!' Amber handed Jake a scraper. 'We've got nothing better to do till we leave tomorrow

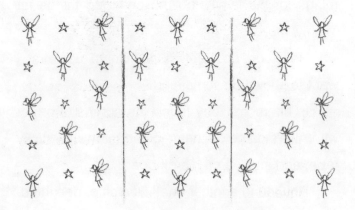

afternoon, so we're all going to exterminate those fairies!'

Toby's eyes shone!

Hours later, when Jake and Amber had gone, Evie and Don came to see how they'd got on.

Toby hugged Evie. 'I'm sorry I was moody, especially after you've done so much for me.'

Don patted him on the shoulder. 'You've done a lot for us, too, lad,' he said.

'Have I?'

Evie nodded. 'Of course you have! You've turned the two of us – Don and me – into a family.'

Toby nearly burst with happiness.

When Don had gone downstairs to start a barbecue, and Evie to burrow in the fridge, Toby went across to his wooden chest. 'I did, once, have a real family,' he said. 'For years, people have asked, "Who's Toby Tucker?", and the answer's in there. I know it is. I just have to keep looking.'

Who will TOBY TUCKER be next?

He's Seti, keeping sneaky secrets in Ancient Egypt!

He's Niko, dodging the donkey doo in Ancient Greece!

He's Titus, sludging through the sewer in Ancient Rome!

He's John Bunn, mucking about with monkeys in Tudor London!

He's Fred Barrow, hogging all the pig swill in wartime London!

EGMONT PRESS: ETHICAL PUBLISHING

Egmont Press is about turning writers into successful authors and children into passionate readers – producing books that enrich and entertain. As a responsible children's publisher, we go even further, considering the world in which our consumers are growing up.

Safety First
Naturally, all of our books meet legal safety requirements. But we go further than this; every book with play value is tested to the highest standards – if it fails, it's back to the drawing-board.

Made Fairly
We are working to ensure that the workers involved in our supply chain – the people that make our books – are treated with fairness and respect.

Responsible Forestry
We are committed to ensuring all our papers come from environmentally and socially responsible forest sources.

For more information, please visit our website at
www.egmont.co.uk/ethicalpublishing